In the
CITY

5.15 a.m.

6 a.m.

To my mum,
who's ninety-seven
and was my
inspiration to draw

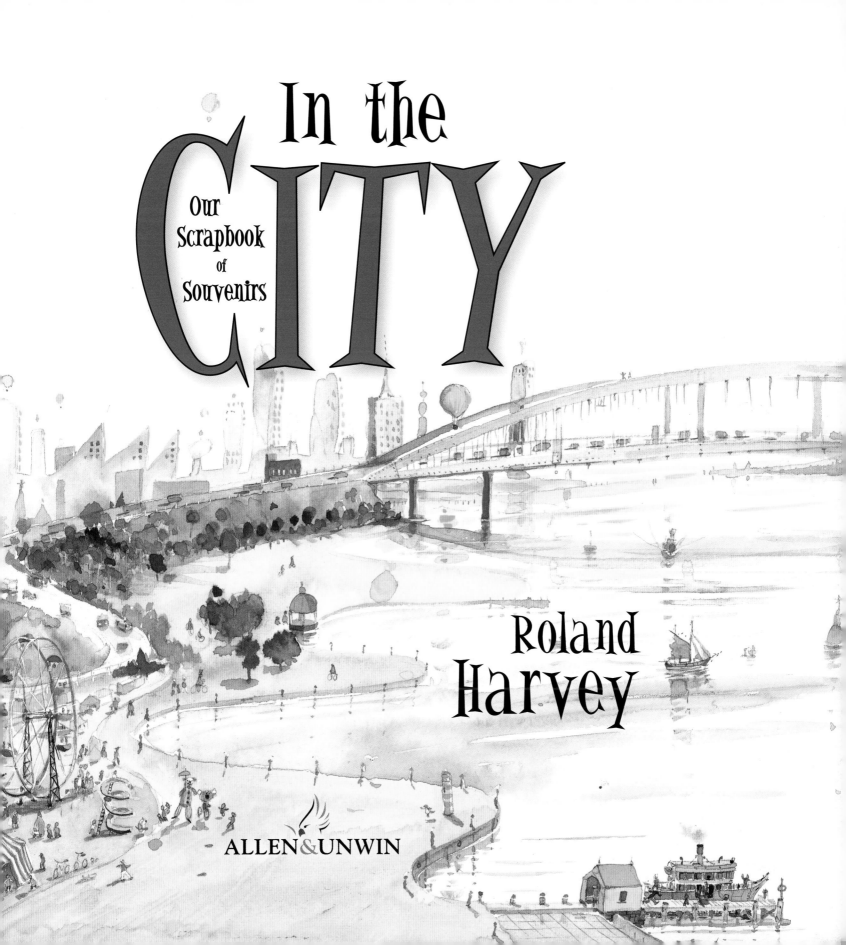

In the
CITY

Our
Scrapbook
of
Souvenirs

Roland
Harvey

ALLEN&UNWIN

Frankie

As we came over the bridge in the shuttle bus, we saw the top of the world's tallest building disappearing into the clouds...and the beach and a Peregrine Falcon and people playing tennis and Luna Park and the zoo and the aquarium.

I saw people going to work

and people going home...

And people parking their cars in the middle of the road.

Dad says there are 3,425,763 people in the city...and us!

And people parking their cars in the middle of the road.

The shuttle bus took us to the world's best hotel: the Grand Palace!

I can't wait to go to the aquarium.

Henry

Uncle Kev says the best way to get the feel of a city is to do a sewer tour... especially when it's raining.

There are hundreds of kilometres of tunnels under the city...

People even live there!

There are tunnels to take cars and trains and gas pipes and power lines and phone lines and water pipes and for people, animals, exhaust fumes, storm water and fresh air.

Sewage goes in as poo and comes out as water for factories and wildlife ponds.

Frankie was scared that all the storm water would wash the fish out of the aquarium before we got there.

At an 'historic' dig' site I bought a dinosaur tooth necklace made from very early plastic.

Penny

The city square was weird at first, but we soon got the hang of it... Uncle Kev said we can go everywhere we want by bus, train, tram and bike, except the toilet.

12·17 p.m. We have seen 3,425,740 people already and a dragon.

We saw university students having coffee and sharing a bowl of pasta.

We bought a T-shirt each and some tricks from a magic shop, but mine disappeared.

It was SO hot today and we went to the COOLEST play at the kids' theatre and then had fish and chips for dinner. Frankie played, 'I want to be a big bad shark,' on the pool-o-phone.

I kept a bottle of shampoo and some shower caps as souvenirs. And a piece of special Grand Palace toilet paper.

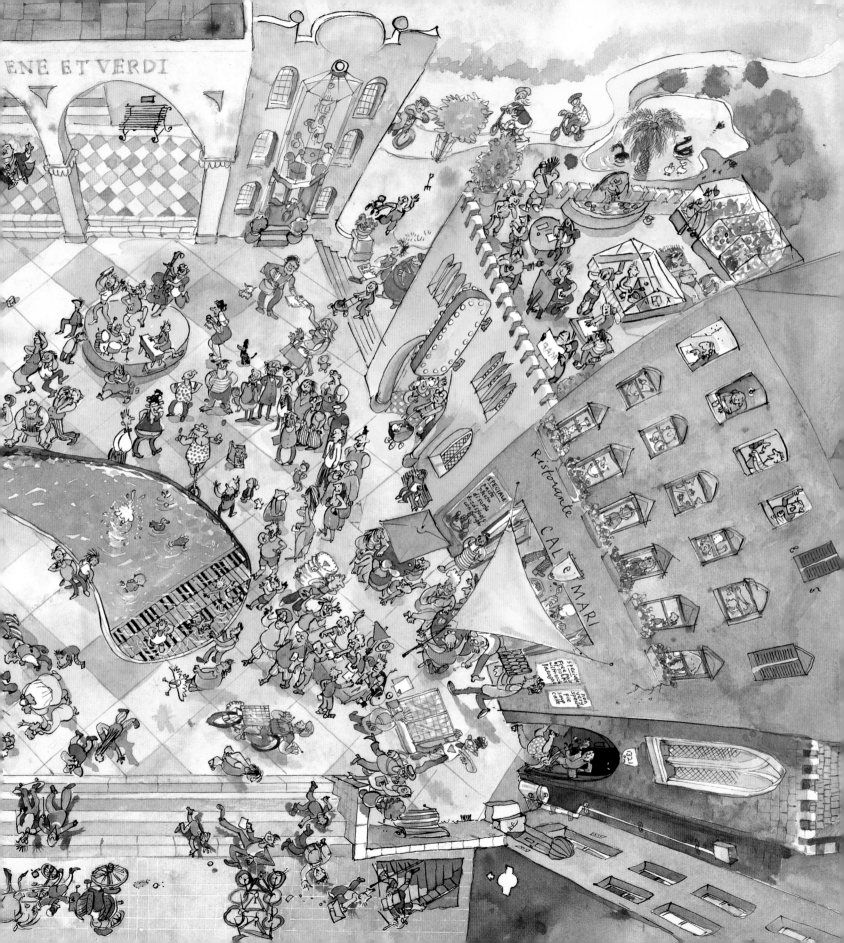

Henry

Our excursion today was to the biggest store in town. I saw some manequins without any clothes on.

SCRAPBOOK
NEWS FLASH

SHOPPERS IN THE CITY WERE SHOCKED TODAY WHEN A TERRIBLE TWO-HEADED BEAST ESCAPED FROM CHANGING ROOMS AND TERRORISED SHOPPERS BEFORE BEING TOLD TO LEAVE THE SHOP.

SIZE 61 →

Frankie and I got squashed in the lift and Penny nearly got crushed in the rush at a book launch.

Frankie said he could see the aquarium from Uncle Kev's office.

Dad and Mum took us for lunch on the roof at Raf's Caf and then picked up a crazy Kombiboard in the Bargain Basement.

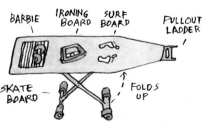

BARBIE   IRONING BOARD   SURF BOARD   PULLOUT LADDER

SKATE BOARD   FOLDS UP

Penny

Zoo checklist:

CATS
- [ ] Tigers
- [ ] Leopards
- [ ] Lions
- [ ] Pumas
- [ ] Ocelots
- [ ] Corgis

NOCTURNAL ANIMALS

MARSUPIALS

PRIMATES
- [ ] Gorillas
- [ ] Orang-utans
- [ ] Chimpanzees
- [ ] Oranges
- [ ] Uncle Kev

ENDANGERED ANIMALS
- [ ] Polar Bears
- [ ] Pandas
- [ ] Animals starting with 'x'

MONOTREMES

BEARS

SEALISH ANIMALS

LONG ANIMALS
- [ ] Giraffes
- [ ] Goannas
- [ ] Pythons
- [ ] Dachshunds

Frankie was disappointed there weren't any sharks.

My souvenir was a really cute little baby Taipan* I found in the toilets.

*Mum said I had to hand it in at the gate.

NOCTURNAL

IN

GIRAFFES ROCK

YOU ARE ON
THE WRONG SIDE
OF THE FEN

Henry

The market is the smelliest place in the world.

It has fishy smells, and mango and banana and old cabbage and herbs and coffee.

We saw a huge crab and tiny silver fish and squid with long tentacles and different coloured prawns and people.

Penny didn't like the meat section because she suffers from Vegetaria. I liked the way the butchers shouted at Mum and Dad. There was stuff even I was allergic to, like gizzards.

I snuck anchovies into Uncle Kev's back pocket.

We bought bread, prawns, nuts, coriander dip, and cow's cheese, goat's cheese, sheep's cheese, lychees and stinky cheese.

Frankie got lost and we found him at the big fish stall.

I got an excellent cheesy souvenir.

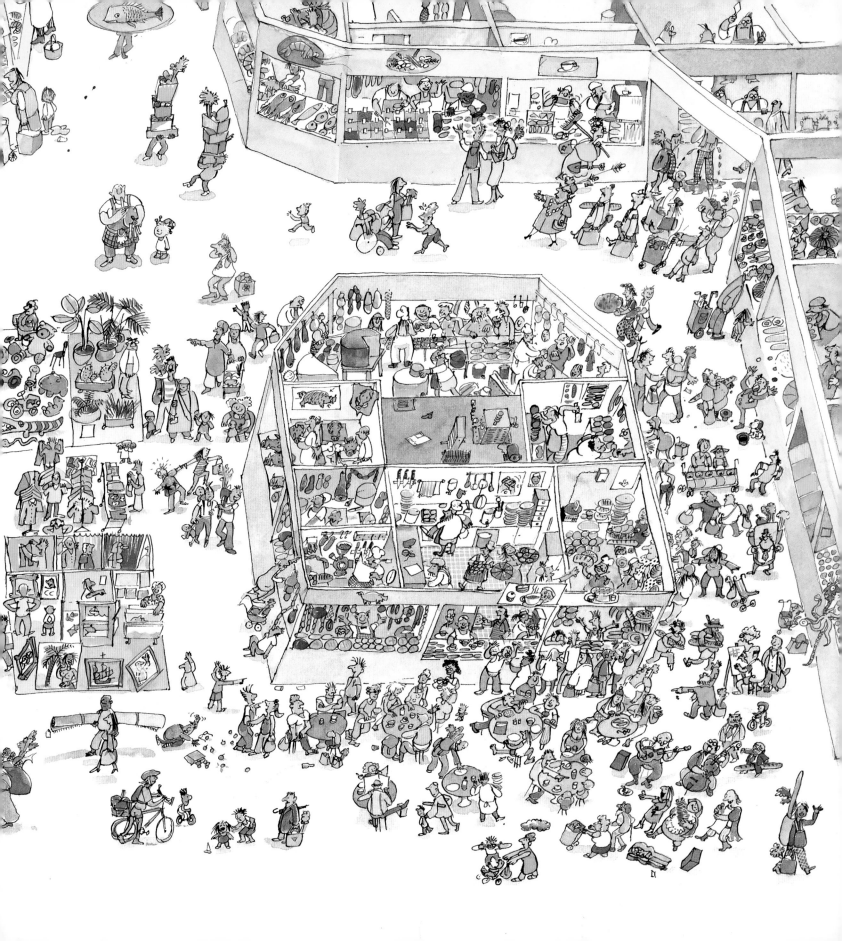

Penny

The Esplanade is where cool people go so you can see them, but Uncle Kev took us anyway as a special treat.

PEOPLE WERE:
Surfing
Cycling
Blading
Watching
Para-surfing   Sailboarding
Kite flying   Jogging
Sleeping
Frisbeeing
Walking
Lying Down

Uncle Kev had a sailboarding lesson and we got to ride in the Rescue Boat.

Mum had raspberry and mango ice-cream. I had beetroot and licorice. Dad had chicken ripple and baci. Frankie had mudcake and Henry had prawn and banana.

Frankie found a crab, but it didn't swim away when he put it in the water, so he kept it as a souvenir.

AND COMMANDO
LESSONS

Henry

Carlington is old and cool. There are bookshops, bike shops, bakeshops, back shops, galleries, cafes, second-hand bookshops, restaurants, gourmet food shops, cookbook shops, arty bookshops and outside toilets.

Uncle Kev's breakdown van broke down.

Penny bought an op-shop wig that makes her look like the Queen.

We walked down the cobbled lanes where they used to take the little cart and empty all the toilets.

Frankie found an antiquarium bookshop.

I found my souvenir at a second-hand bookshop: The Boys' Own Annual from 1946.

Frankie

6.15 a.m. We went
up in a

HOT AIR BALLOON

people
burner
fan
man
envelope
basket
up
down
wind
direction
of travel
FINISH

Uncle Kev explained
how it worked.

When the balloon was going
up it roared like a dragon
and when it was
floating down
it was SILENT!

Penny saw a
frightened swan.

Henry saw
a skate park.

I saw a fox and
undies on a washing line
and a big fish out of water
and a submarine.

BALLOON
ADVENTURER

this is to certify that
Frankie
has successfully
completed a hot air
balloon flight from

We each got
a certificate.

Henry

We went to the toilet at the top of the highest building in the city. It has a glass wall and we could see very strange things...

...like a cinema on the roof!

...and a Peregrine falcon

...and a Peregrine falcon's eggs!

...and a Peregrine shorts

...and window-cleaners!

...and an artist's studio

...and vegie gardens

...and tennis courts

...and Frankie said he could see the aquarium.

We went up and down in the lift eleven times. The tenth time, Dad pushed the buttons for all the floors and a lady got cross.

I found a feather and made a souvenir pen and wrote a letter.

Penny

5 a.m.
I heard sirens and woke up really early.

Henry and I snuck up to the tower at the top of the hotel. We could see flashing lights and smoke and a baker's truck delivering bread, and milk trucks delivering milk,

rubbish trucks delivering rubbish,

water trucks delivering water and burglar trucks collecting burglars

and joggers collecting blisters and a powerful owl.

Frankie slept through the whole thing.

I kept the front page of the newspaper showing the fire.

Henry

The most amazing exhibit at the museum was the giant scientist. We went into his mouth, down his oesophagus... and watched his heart beating 1,2,3 — 1,2,3 — his lungs wheezing and his bowels squeezing.

We even got samples.

I didn't know Indigenous people lived without shops and mobile phones for 50,000 years and they invented barbecues and boats and made mummies before the Egyptians.

Dad said there was a live chameleon in the museum but they can't find it!

Hi! I'm a Chameleon

The bit I liked best was Ned Kelly's iron underpants.

I bought a 3-D pop-up model of the city.

Penny

We went to the oldest part of town which was built before man was invented or cars or electricity or pyjamas.

We saw old stuff like pots and pipes and china and bones and shoes and pistols and dead rats and mugs and T-shirts with pictures of an opera house.

This postcard was from when everything was black and white.

There is a kids' gallery with dress-ups and DVDs of the olden days and you can be an orphan and I saw a chimney-sweep and convicts!

It felt like we had gone back in time, so we had lunch. Frankie was quiet all day – he was saving his energy for tomorrow.

I got a souvenir koala and a photo of some people we don't know.

Frankie

The aquarium! HOORAY!

I saw lots of fish
starting with 's':
sharks, stingrays,
salmon, scallops,
salamanders, sashimi, sea-
snakes, sea slugs, sandwiches
of tuna, sardines,
shrimps, sperm whales,
socktopus, and
a big barracuda.

The divers swam
with the huge sharks
and FED them.

We put our heads in the
bubble and it felt like we
were fish too.

The best animals in
the world are the
leafy sea dragons.

I found out that
barracuda eat anchovies.

Anchovies eat plankton.

Whales and shrimp eat
plankton, too.

Leafy sea dragons eat shrimp and
plankton. They don't eat whales.

I hope nothing eats
leafy sea dragons.

Sharks eat
whatever
they like.

NIGHT, OWEN.
SEE YOU AT
THE PUB LATER

NUH...
I'VE GOT
HOCKEY
PRACTICE...
NITE
PHIL

STAGE
DOOR

First published in 2007

Allen & Unwin
83 Alexander St
Crows Nest NSW 2065
Australia
Phone: (61 2) 8425 0100
Fax: (61 2) 9906 2218
Email: info@allenandunwin.com
Web: www.allenandunwin.com

National Library of Australia
Cataloguing-in-Publication entry:

Harvey, Roland, 1945–.
In the city: our scrapbook of souvenirs.

ISBN 978 1 74114 413 0 (hbk.).

I. Title.

A823.3

Illustration technique: dip pen and watercolour
Designed by Roland Harvey and Sandra Nobes
Typeset in Harvey created by Sandra Nobes from Roland Harvey's handwriting
Printed by Everbest Printing Co., China.
1 3 5 7 9 10 8 6 4 2